Cwtch Me If You Can

Beth Reekles

Published by Accent Press Ltd 2015

ISBN 9781783759354

Printed and bound in the UK

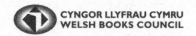
CYNGOR LLYFRAU CYMRU
WELSH BOOKS COUNCIL

Noddir gan
Lywodraeth Cymru
Sponsored by
Welsh Government

Chapter One

Tonight is perfect.

The lighting in Bella Italia is soft and warm, and even though our table is rickety, and my pasta was only lukewarm, tonight is just perfect. At least, *I* think it is. Will keeps fidgeting, like he's nervous, and looking at his watch or around at everyone else.

But, I tell myself, I can't blame him for being distracted. There's a lot to look at. It *is* Valentine's Day, after all, and the restaurant is packed with couples out for a romantic meal together. Most of them are as young as we are.

I've always loved Valentine's Day – the grand gestures to show someone just how much you love them, the 'I love yous'… I smile at Will, thinking how much I love him.

The waiter comes over to ask if we'd like a dessert menu. I open my mouth to say yes, but Will gets there first.

'No, thanks. We're good.'

I try not to let my disappointment show. Maybe Will just has other plans for us and doesn't want to hang around much longer. I bite back a smile, letting my mind wander.

Will clears his throat, like he has something serious to say, and I sit up straighter. Since we started dating, Will's been pretty big on romantic gestures – but he's always excited about them. Never serious. Serious makes me nervous.

I study my boyfriend's face, worry pricking my stomach – suddenly, my spaghetti carbonara isn't sitting so well. Will's brown eyes are looking at the scratch on the table his short fingers are tracing, and his eyebrows are drawn together, tense. His shoulders move up and down and he shifts in his seat.

Has he forgotten his wallet? Maybe he has, and he's worried I'll be upset when he asks me to pay for our romantic meal instead, when he'd promised me that this was his treat.

I couldn't be mad about that. This is *Will*. I love him. We've been going out since we met in September – we were both at the same club, huddled against a wall near the bar because we didn't really like that kind of scene. Our shared hatred of grinding with the other drunk, sweaty people gave us something to talk about – and we hit it off straight away. We've been together ever since.

Aside from how much we have in common, Will's a decent-looking guy. He's got long eyelashes most girls would kill for, and thick blonde hair that sweeps over his face like a guy from a Hollister advert. Although he's not really built like a guy from a Hollister advert.

Will has to know I won't be upset with him for forgetting his wallet.

But as I see how stressed-out and uncomfortable he looks, I start to realise that this is something more serious than him not being able to pay on Valentine's Day.

I bring up a hand to fiddle with the necklace he gave me at Christmas – a slim silver chain with a sterling-silver heart pendant. My heart is in my throat.

'Will,' I say, my voice coming out choked, like I'm about to cry. 'What's going on?'

He sighs. It's a long, tired sigh that fills me with dread. 'Um…'

'Will, just tell me. Whatever it is, I'm sure I can handle it. It'll be fine.' Panic makes my words run together, but I think he understands me.

He's shaking his head. 'This… this is really difficult for me to tell you, Alex, you have to understand that. And I'm – I'm really sorry to have to do this, but… well, I can't do this any more. It's not fair to lead you on.'

Lead me on?

Oh, God, I think, *he isn't… is he?*

But he is.

He's breaking up with me.

On *Valentine's Day*.

Will carries on, but through the blood rushing in my ears, his voice sounds distant. He says how he doesn't feel things are working out between us, that he doesn't see us going anywhere or having much of a future. He says that he knows this must be hard for me to hear, because he knows how much I like him – and he likes me, too…

'I thought you loved me,' I interrupt, my voice a broken whisper. I've been staring blankly at Will as he's been talking, but now I blink, and bring him back into focus. 'I love you. And you've been saying it to me for months.'

'Well…' He clears his throat and pulls at his shirt collar. It's a shirt I bought him for Christmas. 'I – I thought I did, Alex, but I just… can't see us working out. I'm sorry. I don't think it's fair to lead you on,' he tells me again.

'Is there someone else?'

The look on his face tells me everything.

'Oh my God,' I groan, dropping my head into my

hands.

His face turns solemn and intense, and his words are frantic.

'I haven't been cheating on you. I haven't done anything with her, but I - well, I really like her, Alex. I met her at that job interview I went to a couple of weeks ago. You know, the one at the telecom I didn't get? She's so funny, and we both like so much of the same stuff, and...' He trails off, obviously realising how excited he's starting to sound, and he bites his lip.

I narrow my eyes, pulling my hands away from my face – but being careful not to smear the eyeliner I took so much care to put on earlier this evening.

Is he kidding me right now? Like he has nothing in common with *me*? Like I haven't been dating him for the past five months?

My boyfriend – *ex*-boyfriend – is an arse.

I see him looking at his watch again.

'Oh my God,' I say, realising why he's so agitated about what time it is. 'You're going to *meet* her, aren't you, once you get out of here?'

Will, at least, has the grace to blush. 'Um, kind of...'

'Go. Just – *go*.' My voice cracks. I'm on the verge of tears and he will not see me crying over him. I can't even look at him, and I don't want to listen to his pathetic excuses any more. Will scoots his chair back slightly, the legs scraping on the floor with a sharp noise, and then he stops, halfway out of his chair, and I can feel him looking at me.

'Go!' I bark, and he's out of the door in seconds.

My breaths are shallow and shaky, and I know exactly what I need in such a state of distress.

I down my half-full glass of rosé and catch the attention

4

of the waiter who's been serving us all night.

'Can I get the Godfather ice cream sundae please? To share. But just the one spoon.'

Mountains of ice cream and the last half of the bottle of wine later, the restaurant is mostly empty, with a few stragglers holding hands across the table and hunched over so their heads are close together, like they're in their own little bubbles. They all look so in love and sweet.

It makes me feel sick. And, I'm sure, that feeling has nothing to do with all the ice cream I've just eaten.

I can't deny that I'm insanely jealous of all of them.

I mean, never mind the fact that they're all so fricking adorable or that they're spending the night with someone who loves them.

None of them got *dumped* on *Valentine's Day*.

Seriously, I ask myself, who does that? What kind of arsehole do you have to be to break up with your girlfriend on your Valentine's date? *Especially* when she's bought new lingerie for later.

Not that Will knew I'd bought new lingerie. That was supposed to be a surprise for him.

A couple of weeks ago he suggested that we shouldn't do presents for today, and explained that with him 'between jobs' as he put it, and me working and doing classes at the college, we were better off spending our money on a nice night out instead, maybe renting a movie. Now I know better – he didn't want to do presents because he was planning to break up with me.

He must have been planning this for weeks. So why didn't he do it before now? Why did he decide to do it on this, the most sacred romantic night of the year for all couples, of all nights?

My boyfriend – *ex*-boyfriend, I remind myself – is obviously the worst boyfriend in the history of boyfriends.

Maybe I should find out who this 'other girl' is – not to scream at her for stealing my boyfriend, but to let her know what she's letting herself in for.

I order another glass of rosé from a passing waitress, and she gives me a wary look before nodding and bringing me a large glass. I must look crazy, and I can only imagine what they're all muttering about me – the poor girl sitting all on her own drinking too much wine and eating dessert for two, alone on Valentine's, her boyfriend having walked out on her...

They're probably laughing at me back in the kitchen and posting about me on Facebook. They'll probably go see their friends later and tell them all about the sad girl in the restaurant tonight who got dumped.

Looking around again, I see the last two couples – they were double-dating – paying their bill and pulling on their coats. There's a girl behind the bar getting the card machine for them, and my waiter is wiping down tables. Otherwise, it's empty.

I swirl the wine around in the glass and take a gulp. I can barely taste it any more, I've drunk so much of it.

A throat clears.

'Um, can I get you anything else?' the waiter I've had all night asks me. My eyes can't quite focus on him, but I discern that he's got thick, curling brown hair and that he looks very, very sorry for me.

I shake my head, the movement slow and making the room tilt. 'Noooope. Nooo thank you.'

'Is your uh... is your friend not coming back?'

I snort, and then I start crying.

It's not even quiet crying. I'm full-on *bawling*, snot

6

everywhere, and interrupted by hiccups. I snatch up my napkin from my lap, which is stained slightly with chocolate sauce from my ice cream sundae, and blow my nose, wiping away my tears. When I take away the napkin, it's covered in dark foundation and even darker amounts of eyeliner and mascara. If the napkin looks like that, I can only imagine how bad my face looks.

The waiter is still standing by me, holding a little black leather packet in one hand, and shifting his weight uncomfortably from foot to foot. With his free hand, he rubs the back of his neck.

'What do you want?' I ask. Actually, it sounds more like a wail.

He holds out the leather packet. 'It's just that there's the small matter of the bill…'

'The bill,' I repeat, sounding a little more normal now. 'The *bill*.'

'Yes…'

'What's your name?' I slur. He did introduce himself right at the start of the evening, but I barely paid him any attention. I was too wrapped up in Will, and how much I was in love with him, and how perfect the whole night was.

'I'm Sean.'

'I'm Alex. Sit down, Sean.' I pat the table across from me, where Will sat earlier. I gulp some more wine down, and lunge forward, slapping my palm down on the table in front of him. 'Why are all guys such arseholes, Sean?'

'Some guys are,' he agrees, cautiously.

'No, *all* guys. I'm the customer, Sean. The customer is always right. And I'm saying that all guys are arseholes.'

'Um, okay.' He puts the leather packet containing my bill down on the table, off to one side but closer to me than

7

to him. I sniff, and wipe away a few more stray tears with the napkin. 'Do you... do you want to talk about it?'

'He broke up with me on a *date*. On Valentine's Day! And then he went straight to go see this other girl he's had his eye on for weeks. And he doesn't even leave me twenty quid towards his half of the bill.'

'Okay, he does sound like an arsehole. Worse, actually. Any guy with even a little bit of decency would at least pay the bill if he's bringing you on a date just to break up with you.'

'I know! And he was *such* a good guy up until now. He'd buy me flowers, just because, and we'd go try out new restaurants that he'd find, and he got me a spa treatment when I got stressed out with work, and he'd –'

I break off, because I've started crying again.

Sean the waiter leans to the next table and gets a neatly folded napkin from it, and hands it to me. I mumble a thanks, and press it to my eyes, between taking sips of wine. After a few more sips, I manage to stop crying, but the room is sliding out of focus behind Sean.

'Have you got a girlfriend, Sam?'

It sounds more like 'Havooo gat a guuurlfren, Sam?' but he's polite enough not to point out how wasted I am. He does point out that I said the wrong name, though.

'Sean.'

'That's what I said.'

He decides not to argue. 'No, I don't.'

'Well if you did, would you do that to her?'

'No. I think, Alex – it was Alex, right? – that if your boyfriend was a guy like that, you're better off without him. Really. Let this other girl have him and tell him good riddance.'

I touch the necklace Will gave me for Christmas.

'Did he give you that?'

'Yep.'

'You should get rid of it. That's what people do after a bad break-up, isn't it, they purge. They get rid of all the gifts and all the photos and stuff. It makes them feel better. You should get rid of the necklace.'

I think immediately about the lingerie back in my room, and all the tags I cut off. They were an investment, I tell myself, and I can't just throw them out, even if they will forever remind me of tonight.

'Well, don't get rid of them,' Sean the waiter says, and I hear the laugh in his voice.

I think I'm blushing from how humiliating it is that I've just said all that out loud, but I'm not sure. I'm too warm from all the wine so it's hard to tell.

'Just get rid of the necklace,' he says.

I grab the heart pendant and give it a firm yank, like I've seen people do in the movies – but all it does is dig into my neck. 'Owwwww,' I wail, dropping it and massaging the back of my neck with clumsy hands. I can hear Sean the waiter laughing at me, and glare at him.

My lip wobbles.

'Oh, please don't start crying again,' he says, sounding frantic.

'I need a cwtch,' I mumble, thinking about how Will won't be cuddling me to make me feel better about all this. I just need a hug.

'Um…'

'I just want to go *home*.'

Sean leans back. 'Listen, Alex, I'm going to call you a taxi. How about that? And you can go straight home, take a warm bath, sober up, and sleep all of this off. And when you wake up tomorrow you can forget all about him. How does that sound? Does that sound good?'

I nod. 'Okay. Okay.'

He gets up, and I hear him murmuring behind the bar, as I finish my glass of wine. A cup of tea is put down in front of me by the waitress who was hanging around, and she gives me a sympathetic look.

'I'm off, Sean,' she says.

'See you tomorrow,' he calls back to her. I sip the cup of tea, while my head spins and my mind feels foggy, until Sean puts a hand on my shoulder and says, 'Your taxi's here.'

'Thanks.' I get up, but between my brand-new three-inch stilettos that gave me blisters just on the walk from the bus to the restaurant, and the wine, I almost fall over. Sean has to catch my arm and put an arm around my waist to guide me outside. After bundling me into the back of the taxi in a tangle of limbs, heels, and handbag straps, Sean leans in to talk to the driver, and then they ask for my address. I slump in the seat after giving it, and start crying again.

I forget to say thank you to Sean.

When the taxi draws up outside the house I share with three other girls, and I lean forward with my purse open ready to pay, the driver tells me, 'The lad at the restaurant already paid for it, love.'

And that's when I realise I hadn't paid my bill, either.

Chapter Two

On Saturday morning, I wake up fully-clothed, having passed out, lying on my side on my bed. My pastel pink pillowcase is smeared with last night's make-up. My cute red dress that I bought specially for last night's date has ridden up so that it's around my ribs.

I groan, sitting up slowly and wiping a line of drool from the side of my mouth. The room pitches sideways, and I stagger into the bathroom down the hall to throw up, and then retch, until I feel a little less gross.

I clean my teeth, wash off the makeup, change into pyjamas, and stumble back into bed to pass out for a few more hours, hoping to sleep off the hangover that's slowly killing me.

When I wake up again, I feel a little better – until all the memories of the previous night come flooding back to me.

And along with it, the memory that I didn't actually pay for the meal or the taxi.

I should go back to Bella Italia and pay Sean back. I decide to stop by later this week, and spend the rest of the weekend only leaving my room to make cups of tea and to collect a pizza.

Sunday evening, Cathy, my best friend, walks in without bothering to knock.

She's armed with two mugs of tea, and takes one look at my room – used mugs, a half-eaten large pepperoni pizza, dirty clothes scattered around, my stilettos from the other night thrown into the middle of the room… And then she looks at me.

'Oh, *Alex.*'

I haven't looked in the mirror today, but I haven't washed my hair since Friday afternoon, before the disaster that was my Valentine's date, and I've not changed out of my pyjamas since Saturday morning.

Cathy sighs, puts down the tea on some of my many novelty coasters (some people buy pencils or bookmarks when they visit a museum or go on holiday – but I buy coasters), and then marches over to my window, throwing open the curtains.

I cringe from the light – the sun is setting, and the amber glow is just hitting my window. I pull the covers up over my head, only for Cathy to yank them back. She stands amongst my dirty clothes, hands on hips, pursing her lips and looking just like her mother.

'You look like your mum,' I tell her.

'And you,' she replies bluntly, 'look like hell.'

'I got dumped on Valentine's Day,' I tell her, like she doesn't already know. I bet everyone knows – I mean, how many people get dumped on Valentine's Day anyway? 'I'm allowed to look like hell. I have no faith in romance any more.'

I try to pull my sheets and duvet back from her, but fail. So, I lean down and reach for another piece of pizza. A loose bit of pepperoni falls onto my pyjama shorts, and I pick it up quickly, popping it into my mouth. There's a faint, greasy red mark left, though. *Damn, that's going to stain.*

Cathy, my best friend and stand-in mother while I'm living with her, huffs. She's only wearing leggings and an old *Wicked!* t-shirt, blonde hair pulled back in a plait, but she looks way better than I imagine I do.

'Help yourself,' I say, after swallowing, gesturing at the pizza box on the floor.

She shakes her head at me. 'You have work at nine a.m. tomorrow, Al. You've got to pull yourself together. Shit happens. People break up. And, let's face it, Will wasn't even that attractive.'

'He *was*.'

Cathy snorts. 'Maybe to you. You were in love with him. But his ears were too big, his eyes were too close together, he was always bringing dirt into the house because he'd never wipe his feet on the mat outside. He dropped out of his one single college class, because his FIFA football team was more important than his homework. And he was too lazy to even *try* to get a job after he got fired from the last one. He didn't even like drinking tea, for God's sake!'

Now it's my turn to purse my lips. Okay, so maybe she has a point (or several) but it still hurts that Will dumped me so brutally. I loved him. Love wasn't a switch I could just turn off because we weren't together any more.

And I know that Cathy's just trying to help me, make me feel better. Her methods seem a little harsh to me right now, but I know I'll thank her later. I always do.

'Well, not everyone likes tea.'

My best friend rolls her eyes. 'You're ridiculous, Alex. Face it – Will was a loser, and you were too in love with him to see it. Pull yourself together.'

'But I loved him,' I moan. 'I need time to heal.'

Cathy smiles at me fondly, sitting on the edge on my bed. She's always telling me that I'm too much of a romantic, and that I need to 'check back into reality'. She has had a couple of boyfriends, but I don't think she's ever actually been in love.

'You don't understand,' I insist.

'I understand that he was a loser and that you deserve better, and that whoever this other girl is, she'd better hope he doesn't treat her like that, too. And I understand that you have work tomorrow that you cannot be late for.'

'What's that got to do with it, *Mum*?'

'I'm just saying.' Her voice is softer now, and she tucks a loose strand of hair behind her ear. 'You can't mope around here forever. We're watching *Hollyoaks* after tea, so get up, wash your hair, clean up in here a bit, and come down to watch it with us. And for God's sake, put those pyjamas in the wash. They'll stink.'

'They don't stink…'

'It smells like something died in here,' she tells me.

'All my hope and belief in true love and romance died. Have some compassion.'

Cathy laughs, then opens my windows wide and sprays some of my perfume into the air before picking up her mug of tea and leaving me.

I want to pull the covers back up over my head and sleep until I have to get up for work tomorrow morning, but I know that Cathy's right. She's *always* right.

Cathy and I have been friends since our GCSE years, when we were the only two girls in our small Spanish class.

Everyone always said we're like chalk and cheese – I act on impulse and follow my gut, but Cathy likes to think out every possible consequence of her actions before doing anything. I fall in love, Cathy does not. Cathy can cook, and I defrost ready meals in the microwave. I've got dark skin, thanks to some Indian heritage on my dad's side, and Cathy's so fair that she burns even in a little bit of sunshine.

But we've been firm friends for years, in spite of all that.

I'd been terrified when Cathy told me she was going to Cardiff University, studying French and German. I'd dropped out of Sixth Form by then because I was struggling too much, and I'd picked up a job in Tesco instead. I panicked that she'd move on with her life at uni and forget all about me.

But Cathy wasn't about to leave me behind. She was the one who convinced me to move in with her and two other girls in their second year of uni, and to start going to some college classes. She's always believed in me way more than I believe in myself.

The two other girls we live with, Ellie and Julia, shared a flat with Cathy during her first year. The guys they lived with were absolute pigs, I'm told, so the girls bonded and got a house together for this year without them.

So once I've done as Cathy said, and cleaned myself and my room up, I go downstairs to watch *Hollyoaks*.

'Thank God,' Cathy says, as I join them. 'I thought we were going to have to go up and pull you out of your pit of self-pity.'

'I'm fine,' I sigh. 'Just, you know, heartbroken.'

'Always with the melodrama,' laughs Julia. But then her face turns serious, and her mouth twists in sympathy. She tucks her legs up beneath her on the sofa. 'You were a mess when you got home. I've never seen you that badly drunk before.'

'Mmph.'

Usually I handle my drink better; I know when to switch to a soft drink and leave the alcohol alone. But

Friday night, I'd drunk that rosé with reckless abandon.

'Seriously, I know it was rough, being Valentine's Day, and all, but –'

'But *nothing*, Jules,' Ellie interrupts, jumping to my defence before I can speak for myself. 'The slime-ball went straight to jump into bed with that other girl.'

'We don't *know* that they were having sex,' Cathy calls from the kitchen, where she's making tea for us all, ever the voice of reason. 'I mean, we don't even know who she is.'

'How much *do* you know about her?' Julia asks, forgetting to be gentle and feel sorry for me, and getting excited. 'Maybe we can find her on Facebook.'

'We are not looking up *the other woman* on Facebook,' Ellie snaps, rolling her eyes. 'We're turning a blind eye to Alex's ex-boyfriend for the next hour and watching *Hollyoaks*. Okay?'

'Okay, okay,' Julia mumbles. She gives me a smile like we are sharing a secret, rolling her eyes at Ellie, and then wanders out into the kitchen to help Cathy bring the tea in.

I manage to forget about Will for the next hour, but afterwards, I think out loud, 'I should go back to Bella Italia tomorrow, to try and find that guy.'

'What guy?' Jules asks, her tired, drooping eyes snapping open.

'There's *another* guy?' Cathy sounds like she is totally fed up with me, and disbelief is written all over her face. But she smiles at me a little. 'Christ, and I thought you were too hung up on Will to even notice anyone else.'

'There's not a guy, exactly,' I try to explain. 'It's just – the waiter, from the restaurant. Sean. He sort of sat with me while I was crying over Will and sorted me out a taxi home.'

16

'That was good of him,' Ellie says. 'But why do you need to find him?'

'He paid for the taxi home for me. And I was so drunk I forgot about paying the bill for the meal – and with three courses and all the wine, it won't have been cheap. I should go back and, you know, sort it out. Pay him back.'

I see the other girls exchanging glances. Julia speaks: 'This guy sounds like your knight in shining armour, Al.'

'Shining armour,' I say, 'or a dirty apron.'

Reasons to Never Ever Ever Date Again

- It'll take a long time to get over Will
- Guys are idiots
- They will break up with me on romantic dates
- They will break my heart and probably never think about me again
- Romance is dead

Chapter Three

When I'm not reading cheesy romance novels or trying to do my coursework, I work in one of the many Starbucks in Cardiff. Sometimes the customers can be annoying, but it pays okay, and I love the smell of fresh coffee.

It's Wednesday afternoon, and slow. There's a guy in the corner by the window on a laptop, a couple of girls at a table catching up with each other, and a middle-aged couple with a few John Lewis carrier bags.

I slump against the counter, sighing heavily. Cerys, the other girl working with me at the moment, knows all about me and Will. A friend of hers was at Bella Italia on Friday and saw the whole thing.

Talk about humiliating.

And to make things worse, she hasn't shut up about it. I've asked her to stop, but she's relentless. She's been with her girlfriend for four years, so I think she must love hearing other people's love-life dramas.

And she wants to know all about the other girl. She's itching to go onto Will's Facebook page and try to figure out who the girl he left me for is. Not in a mean way, just nosy.

I tell her about Sean the waiter, too. I don't mention what nice hair he had, but when she asks me if he was fit, I shrug and say, 'I guess.'

I'd tried to find him on Monday – I went into Bella Italia in the early evening and asked if he was working. He wasn't.

'It's just,' I said, 'I was here on Friday, and I sort of accidentally left without paying, and…'

'Oh. You're the girl who got dumped, aren't you?'

My cheeks flamed. 'Yes. That's me. And I wanted to pay what I owe –'

'Sean already settled the bill for you.'

'That's very generous of him, but –'

'You'll have to take it up with Sean.'

'Well,' I sighed, 'could you tell me when he's working?'

'Not until Thursday.'

Since I haven't got any other way to contact him, I make the decision to go back again on Thursday to pay him back. I should've asked for his last name. Then I could've looked him up on Facebook, and tried to contact him that way.

The door opens, and Cerys and I both stand up straight.

It's two guys and a girl, around my age, and they browse the baked treats before shuffling up, one by one, to the counter, giving Cerys their orders to-go and waiting for me to make them up.

When I finish the third drink, I turn to put it down on the counter.

'Latte, extra espresso,' I say, handing it to the guy. He looks familiar, but I can't place him… I guess I've probably seen him around the town some time.

'Hey,' he says brightly, like he knows me, or something. 'Alex.'

I frown at him, racking my brain trying to figure out who the hell this guy (this very attractive guy, I might add) is. 'Um, yeah… Sorry, who are you?'

His left eyebrow quirks up. 'You don't recognise me?'

I frown deeper, squinting at him, and thinking harder. 'Sorry. No. Did we maybe… meet at a party, or something?' I'm trying to think where he might know me from. Is he one of Will's friends? Is he in my college class?

He doesn't look disappointed, though, just smiles wider. *God, that smile could make a girl swoon*, I think.

Thick, brown hair with slight curls in sexy disarray, and bright green eyes. He's got glasses on – rectangular black frames that suit him well – and he looks incredible in a green jumper and worn jeans. He looks like a guy you'd be happy to take home to meet your parents. Cathy would most definitely approve.

His eyes flicker down, to the open neck of my blouse, and for a minute I think he's actually being a prat to look so obviously at my cleavage, until he says –

'You're still wearing it.'

'Wearing what?'

'The necklace.'

I touch a hand to my necklace. Even if I'm mad at Will, I haven't got over him just yet.

Then something slides into place in my brain.

'*Ohmigod*. Sean?'

'Ah.' He flashes me that smile again. 'So you do remember me.'

'God. Oh, my God. Listen, I'm so sorry about Friday night. I didn't mean to, you know, hijack your night when you were working, or anything, and I'm sorry for being such a pain. And you have to let me pay you back for the taxi and the food. I tried to find you Monday at the restaurant but they told me you weren't working until tomorrow…'

I stop for air, having talked a mile a minute, and Sean

21

laughs. It's a deep, low laugh that makes my belly feel warm and full of butterflies.

'Don't worry about it. You were having a really rough night, and I'm glad I could help.'

'Seriously, though, you have to let me pay you back. How much was it? I have some cash in my purse, so I can pay you back at least a bit now, and I can bring you the rest tomorrow, when you're working, or –'

'Really, don't worry. I'll consider it a Good Samaritan act,' he jokes. 'Use it to build up my good karma.' He lifts his latte toward me in a gesture like he's going to say 'cheers'. 'I'll catch you round, Alex.'

'See – see you round,' I stammer in reply, watching him go back to his friends near the door, and they all leave.

Cerys grabs me by the shoulders, giving me a little shake. 'That boy could not be any cuter if he tried.'

'Oh, I don't know about that…'

'Why didn't you give him your number? Even if you don't want to go out with him, that's the kind of guy you want to keep around. Or you should've asked for his number.'

'I told you earlier – I've sworn off all guys.'

'Sweetie, he wasn't just a guy. He was a *god*. I can still appreciate an attractive guy when I see one.'

I snort, shaking my head at her.

I've promised myself I won't date again for a while, until I'm properly over Will, and Sean is exactly the kind of guy who would make me forget about that promise. It's a good thing I'll probably never see him again.

Chapter Four

The lights flash between white and blue and purple, and back again. I bounce on my feet, body swaying side to side, and sigh. Cathy doesn't notice. She's got her arms above her head, hips sashaying in time with the music, eyes drooping from adrenaline and alcohol. I have no idea where Ellie and Julia have buggered off to, but I wish they'd come back. If they've gone home and left me here, I'll kill them.

Some guy sidles up behind me, puts his hands on my hips and pulls me against him.

Reason five billion and seven why I hate clubbing.

I peel his hands off me, glaring at him over my shoulder. He just smiles back, not getting the message. Great. Just what I need. I tell him where to go, shouting to be heard over the pounding music, and he holds his hands up in surrender, stumbling back a step.

'Whoa, chill out,' he slurs, but walks away.

I grab Cathy's arm to get her attention, and her eyes snap open, taking a few seconds to focus on me. 'I'm going outside. I need some air.'

'Okay. I'll be at the bar. Come find me there. Do you want me to get you another drink?'

Another drink would make this more bearable, but I'm not in the mood for it. I tell her so, and she nods, walking with me halfway before I head off toward the doors. I have to elbow my way through swarms of people crowding to get to the bar or the dance floor, but eventually I break out into the cold night air, and gulp down a big breath.

It's the last Saturday before Easter, late in March. Next weekend, most people will be going home. The uni students will have finished lectures for the term, and people in work will be making the most of the bank holiday to go see their families or take a well-earned break. This is the last chance most of us have to go out with our friends until after exams.

And even though it has been almost two months since Will broke up with me, it still stings. I'm still swearing off all guys, much to Cathy's surprise. Will has ruined any belief I had in romance.

I wrap my arms around myself, teeth chattering from the cold. I am only wearing shorts and a red silky camisole, and now, away from all the sweaty, dancing people back inside, I'm *freezing*.

I start to debate going back inside, or maybe just going home, when a voice interrupts my thoughts.

'Not your sort of thing either, huh?'

I look over to my left, and my jaw drops. He is smiling shyly, pushing back his hair with one hand and messing it up, as he steps closer to me.

'Sean,' I choke out. 'Hi.'

Okay, so even if I *have* promised myself I'm not going to date any other guys for a long while yet, I've been keeping an eye out for Sean. I reckon he must be studying at Cardiff. But it's a big place, and it's not *that* easy to just run into someone.

Which has either been really lucky, or unlucky.

He's been back into my Starbucks a few times – twice when we were so busy I could only throw him a fleeting smile before making up more orders, and a couple of times when I wasn't there. Cerys would tell me the next time we were on together, 'Your fit friend came in the other day.'

'Did he ask about me?' I couldn't help myself.

'He just said, 'I guess Alex isn't on today.' And I said, 'Nope.''

Other than that, I haven't seen him.

And now he's *here*, of all places, when I have hair sticking to the back of my neck and probably stink of booze and sweat from just being in the club. I can hardly believe it.

Sean, of course, looks drop-dead gorgeous again.

'Not your kinda thing?' he asks again.

'Not really. What about you?'

'I don't mind it, but I was kind of hoping to have a quiet night in.'

'With your girlfriend?' I blurt, unable to stop myself.

He laughs. 'No, with an essay I've got due in. God, that makes me sound like a loser, doesn't it?'

'No, not at all,' I say quickly, even though Julia would agree with him. 'I'm only here because my mates dragged me out.'

'Same.' He leans one shoulder against the wall, his body turned towards me.

'So how did they bribe you to come out?' I ask. 'My friends promised to buy my drinks all night.'

'Well they didn't so much bribe me, they just...' He sighs, then smiles sheepishly at me. 'It's my birthday. And somehow they talked me into coming out to celebrate, rather than writing an essay.'

'Oh.' I bite my lip but say, 'Well, uh, happy birthday!'

'Thanks.'

'How old are you?' I ask, before I can wonder if that's too rude to ask because really, when you think about it, I barely know him.

25

'Twenty-two,' he grumbles.

'And you didn't want to celebrate?'

'My idea of celebrating doesn't really include clubs.' He eyes the doorway behind us, his gaze trailing up to the roof, and his lips curl in distaste.

'Well, what does it include?'

Screw this whole thing of swearing off guys – I might not be the romantic I used to be, but hell, I am *not* passing up the opportunity to flirt with a guy as sexy as Sean when he's giving me the chance.

His eyes meet mine and for a second, I'm totally dumbstruck, and my legs feel like jelly. Is this what swooning feels like? If it is, then I'm swooning.

He leans toward me slightly – not like he's going to kiss me or anything, but like he's going to speak more softly, more intimately.

Up this close, I notice that his eyes aren't just green, but have flecks of gold in them.

And just when I thought he couldn't get any more gorgeous, he says, 'Do you want to get out of here?'

Definitely swooning now.

Before I can respond, hands grab my shoulder and forearm, and Cathy leans up against me, head on my shoulder. 'You're not going home, are you?'

I push her up so she's standing more on her own feet. Her eyes are wide, but glazed-over slightly, and her smile is wide and expectant. 'Where's Jules and Ellie?' I ask.

'Oh, they're inside. They were in the loos.' Her words are slurred, and when she says 'loos' it comes out more like 'looooooooos.'

'So they're staying with you?'

'Uh-huuuuuuh.'

'I think we were just about to head somewhere else,'

26

Sean pitches in, stepping out from the wall to get Cathy's attention. His eyes flicker back to me. 'Unless you'd rather stay here with your mates?'

'Wait,' Cathy says, sounding a little more sober now. Her eyes narrow at Sean. 'Don't I know you?'

'Um, I don't know.'

She squints at him more, then squeals. 'Ooh! Ooh, I know how I know you! Aren't you like, treasurer or something for the French society?'

'Yeah, that's me.'

Cathy's mouth opens slightly as if she's about to say something to me, but then she looks back at Sean, and her eyes widen even further. Her mouth slides very slowly back shut. 'Right. Okay.' She hiccups. 'I'll leave you to it. Don't do anything I wouldn't do.'

My best friend skips back inside the club, shooting me a grin over her shoulder, and winking. I want to turn to dust and blow away in the wind, I'm so embarrassed.

Sean doesn't seem to notice. He just smiles easily at me, and says, 'Your friend?'

'Best friend. And she kind of acts like mum in our house. Fixing holes in pockets and making sure we've got enough dish-washer tablets and paracetamol in the cupboards, you know.'

Sean laughs. 'In that case, I'm probably house-mum. I'm always doing stuff like that.'

I smile, and then, because it looks like we're going somewhere together – and not back into the club – I say, 'So, where are we going?'

We end up in McDonalds.

Hardly glamorous, I know, but it's not like there are any coffee shops open right now, and most of the pubs are rowdy and near closing. So we're sitting in the too-bright light of McDonalds, opposite each other at a table near the window, with fries and cups of tea between us.

And I can't think of a single thing to say to him. I know this isn't a date, but still…

'You're not wearing that necklace,' he says, filling the silence.

'You're not wearing your glasses,' I respond.

'Contacts. They're easier on a night out. Did you get rid of it? The necklace, I mean.'

I touch a hand to my naked throat. 'No. It's buried in my jewellery box.'

'Well, that's better than still wearing it.' He smiles.

'I'm still not really over him.'

I'm such an idiot! Was that a good thing to say? Is he going to run a mile now because he thinks I'm one of those girls who obsesses over an ex-boyfriend?

But hey – he brought it up.

I bite my lip, looking away from him out of the window. I hope I'm not blushing. And I hope he doesn't think I'm as big an idiot as I feel.

'Um, so,' he says, 'What do you do? Is Starbucks the future for you? I feel really weird, because we've met a few times, but I still don't actually know much about you.'

Glad of the change of topic, I turn back to him, wrapping my hands around my cup of tea. 'Okay, well, I dropped out of Sixth Form after barely passing my AS Levels, worked in Tesco and a pub for a bit. Now I'm doing some college courses in psychology. What about you?'

'Fourth year French,' he answers. 'I spent my third year abroad. Probably going to go into teaching.'

'So you know what you want to do with your life.'

'Kind of. At least, I'd like to get the qualifications to be a teacher, so I can go into it if I want to. What do you want to do?'

I laugh, so hard that I give the most unattractive snort. 'I have no clue.'

He shrugs. 'That's okay. I have mates who still don't know what they want to do.'

And after that, talking with Sean is easy. I tell him more about me – like how I quit Sixth Form because I thought I'd never get my grades up (and how Cathy was the one who convinced me to give college a try and not give up on myself), and how I passed my driving test first time with only two minors.

I learn that Sean's dad is Irish – but his parents had a rough divorce when he was little, so he only sees his dad a couple of times a year because he lives in York now, and Sean and his mum and little sister live in Swansea. He tells me that he broke his arm falling out of a tree when he was fourteen, that he took three tries to pass his driving test, and my jaw drops when I hear about the two A* grades he got at A Level.

'You probably could've got into Oxbridge.'

'I didn't bother applying. It would've been too much pressure.'

'Fair enough.'

We talk about music, movies, TV shows we like, and when we realise we both love watching *Game of Thrones* (but he's read the books and I haven't) we talk about that for about twenty minutes, mostly debating over Sansa Stark's character.

Being with Will used to be easy because we liked so much of the same stuff, and we were so alike. And even though Sean and I have things in common, it's different –

it's like almost everything he says is a surprise to me. And that's good.

But I'm not going to start dating him, I remind myself. I won't. I'm not in the right place to do that. Emotionally or mentally. I need a break from dating. And with my disastrous history when it comes to romance, I'm starting to convince myself that I must be jinxed.

We spend almost two hours in McDonalds.

If I'm honest, it's was a much better way to spend my night than pushing away drunk, groping guys under strobe lighting.

I'd stay longer with Sean, but we're both starting to yawn. And I know that if I spend too much longer with him, I'm at a serious risk of forgetting about my ban on boys.

Just as I'm wondering how to tell him I want to head back home, I'm saved by the bell: my phone starts to ring.

I give Sean a look that says 'sorry', and answer. It's Julia.

'Where are you?' She's shouting, and I can hear other voices in the background calling to each other, and, behind that, music with heavy bass and some guy rapping over the top of it.

'Nice talking to you, too. I'm in McDonalds.' I tell her which one, describing where I am. 'Are you still at the club?'

'We're just about to call a taxi. Are you getting one with us? Or going back to Lover Boy's?'

'He's not –' I break off, blushing. I can't call Sean 'Lover Boy' (whether he is or not) when he's right there in front of me, hearing my every word. I just hope he can't hear Julia. Self-conscious, I press the button on the side of my phone to turn down the volume.

'I'll meet you guys and come back with you,' I tell her instead. 'Where are you?'

When I hang up, Sean smiles easily at me, and starts to stand. 'I'll walk you back to meet your mates.'

'Oh, you don't have to do that.'

His smile turns to a smirk. 'Can't have a pretty girl wandering around all on her own. Come on. Where are you meeting them?'

'Maddison,' I tell him, picking up my bag and slinging the strap across my body. I try not to think too much about the fact that he just called me pretty. 'You really don't have to walk me there, you know. I don't mind if you'd rather go find your own mates.'

He shrugs. 'They'll be fine without me.'

'But it's your birthday.'

'Actually, it's after midnight, so not any more.'

I roll my eyes, waving a hand in a 'whatever' gesture. 'Details.'

'That's them.' I point to where Julia, Ellie and Cathy are huddled together on the pavement near a phone box. Jules is on her phone, and Cathy is chatting to Ellie. We've stopped at the end of the road, and there are so many people around on the pavements that they haven't seen me yet.

I turn back to Sean, and smile, but it feels stiff, almost formal. Suddenly, everything feels awkward. The air is thick, like it's charged with tension that doesn't know where to go. The kind of weird and awkward tension that I recognise from the end of first dates with boys when you don't know whether to kiss them or hug them or just call 'bye' and walk away.

Only this isn't a date.

And I'm *not* going to kiss him.

Besides, Sean was probably just being nice. He didn't want to go clubbing, saw an easy escape with me for a few hours, and that's all it was. I bet the last thing on his mind is dating me, when he saw me in such a state back on Valentine's Day.

I bite my lip, though, because in spite of what I tell myself, I'm nervous.

Sean clears his throat. He obviously feels the suspense between us too. 'Thanks for tonight. I had a really great time.'

'Me, too.'

I can practically hear crickets chirping in the silence that follows.

'Um…' He clears his throat again. God, I think Sean's even more nervous than I am. 'So, I guess, I'll maybe, um, see you around, some time?'

'Sure.'

Then the girls notice me, because over the din of people on a night out and the music spilling out of the open doors of the clubs along the road, I can hear Cathy shouting, 'Alex! Alex! Alex, over here!'

'I'd better go.'

'Sure.' Sean rubs the back of his neck, and then before I can turn away, he ducks down to kiss me on the cheek. I jump back, totally startled. 'Bye, Alex. Have a good Easter.'

'You – you too,' I stammer, and blink at him a few times before walking to meet my friends. When I meet them, I can hear them talking to me, but I can't focus. I'm too stunned. Instead, I just lift a hand to touch my cheek where he kissed me, and look back over my shoulder to see Sean raise a hand to me in farewell.

Reasons to want to date Sean

- He's the most handsome guy in the history of guys
- He might like me
- Even after seeing me in a state on Valentine's Day he hasn't ignored me
- He seems like a really, really great guy
- He's funny
- He's smart
- He's kind
- Did I mention how good-looking he is yet?

Reasons not to date Sean

- Dating is a bad idea right now
- He kissed me on the cheek and that means he's probably not actually interested
- There's no way he's interested. He was just being nice.
- I'm not really over Will
- I'll get my heart broken. I always do.

Chapter Five

Two days later, Cathy and I are both at the house for a couple of hours, before I have to go to work. The other two girls are still at classes.

I managed to avoid most of their questions on Saturday night (or, rather, Sunday morning). I dismissed it, saying we were friends and that was all.

Cathy isn't falling for it, though. She knows me too well.

She hasn't mentioned to Julia or Ellie that she knows Sean the waiter from university, and I'm glad. It's hard enough to get my feelings straight in my head without a bunch of other people pitching in.

Right now, we're sitting in the living room with some left-over Chinese takeaway we all ordered yesterday, *Deal or No Deal* playing on the TV. We're not paying any attention to it though – instead, my best friend is finding out everything from my night with Sean.

I have to tell her. She's my best friend. I can't hide stuff from her. And even if I don't want everyone's advice, I'd like to talk to someone about it. And even if Cathy hasn't been in love, she's realistic when it comes to relationships.

'I can't believe I know him,' she says for the billionth time. 'How crazy is that? I mean, I don't know him *that* well. But I've talked to him a little on society pub crawls and stuff like that. I mean, he seems like a nice guy.'

'He is.'

She rolls her eyes, shovelling more sweet and sour

chicken into her mouth. She says, mouth full, 'So tell me again what happened at the end of the night?'

I sigh, poking the noodles in my plastic tub. 'He walked me round to Maddison to meet you, and then it got all awkward as we were saying goodbye. Like, end-of-a-first-date awkward. And he said he had a nice time, and I said that I did too, then you called me, and he just – just kissed my cheek.'

Cathy frowns, swallowing. 'And you're totally sure he wasn't aiming for your mouth and missed?'

'Definitely not.'

'A kiss on the cheek?'

'Like a peck. Like you'd kiss your gran at Christmas.'

My best friend sighs heavily, shaking her head. 'Boys are a goddamn mystery.'

'This is why,' I say, 'I'm not dating. For a while.'

'But you like this guy.'

I groan, thinking about the lists I made to try to help me answer that same question, putting my half-eaten leftovers back on the coffee table and tucking my feet up under me on the sofa. I pull a cushion onto my lap. 'I don't know, Cathy. I mean, he's a hard guy not to like. He's just got that kind of personality. And, of course, he's totally gorgeous.'

'And he must like you.'

I shrug. 'Yeah, enough to hang out with me. But he probably just likes me as a friend, or something.'

'But –'

'Otherwise,' I interrupt, 'he'd have actually tried to kiss me on Saturday.'

'Mm.' She can't disagree with that, so she doesn't. And she doesn't try to offer me any advice on it, either. We both turn back to *Deal or No Deal*, just as someone opens the 1p box and everyone celebrates.

Out of the corner of my eye, I see Cathy smile at the TV. I don't. I can't really concentrate on the telly anyway. I'm too busy replaying Saturday night with Sean in my head again.

Before Will destroyed all my faith in romance, I'd have said that there was a spark when Sean kissed my cheek. That my skin was tingling afterwards from the imprint of his lips. That we had *chemistry*.

But now, I just think maybe that spark I felt was because it was so cold, and his lips were warm.

There's nothing romantic between us. The only reason he kissed my cheek is to make a point that whatever there is between us, it's just friendship.

There's no real reason we keep running into each other, either. I can't believe it's fate pushing us together. There's no such thing as fate.

And in spite of what I tell myself, I can't help but feel a little sad about that.

When I get home from work later that day, I find myself rooting out the shoeboxes from under my bed. The first shoebox used to hold the Converse I bought in the January sales, but inside is what would look to anyone else like a pile of rubbish.

It's not rubbish, though. It's all my mementoes from my last relationship. Cinema tickets, receipts from meals, photos I'd printed to put on my pin board. I go to my jewellery box, take out the necklace Will gave me that's buried there, and drop it into the shoebox, too.

I think I'm finally ready to move on. Or at least try to move on.

I pull out the other shoeboxes, then, and line them up in

front of me on the floor.

I have had four boyfriends in my life.

The first was when I was ten. It started at the last school disco of Year Six, before we all left for comprehensive school. Barry Jones gave me his Penguin biscuit, and then we danced the *Cha-Cha Slide* together, and at the end of the disco he asked if I wanted to be his girlfriend.

We went to the cinema twice (once over the summer, once at Christmastime), both times with one of our parents in tow. We bought each other presents on holidays and gave each other Easter eggs.

And sometimes we held hands in the school yard and once, on Valentine's Day at school in Year Seven, he kissed me on the lips for a dare.

He broke up with me at the start of Year Eight, when he realised that other girls were starting to develop noticeable boobs and I looked more like a boy, with my short bob and flat chest.

That was the first time I got my heart broken. I cried all night and my mum told me, 'You'll get your heart broken plenty of times before you find the boy who pieces it all back together for you.'

I hadn't believed her. I always thought that I would only ever fall for The One.

The One being the guy I would want to spend my whole life with. My knight in shining armour, my Prince Charming, my soulmate.

I take the lid off the shoebox, looking at the rope bracelets of beads that Barry gave me as holiday presents, the tickets from the two movies we went to see, and a few photos.

I wiggle the lid back onto the box, and move on to the

next one.

My second boyfriend was the boy I fancied all of Year Nine, once I'd overcome my first bout of heartbreak. His name was Lorenzo – but everyone called him Ren. He was one of the coolest guys in our school year, and all the girls fancied him because he was exotic. His mum was Spanish and he took after her, with thick, shiny black hair and high cheekbones and olive skin.

He asked me out at a birthday party mid-way through the school year, and our romance was intense and brief. There was a lot of snogging in the school corridors in the gaps between lockers at lunchtime, when there wasn't anyone around. And snogging at birthday parties we were both invited to. And snogging in the park, because all the cool kids hung out in the park in the evening on a Friday night.

It ended when Ren moved back to Spain before the start of the next school year, and my heart was broken once again.

My shoebox with reminders of that relationship contains less than the first one. There are only a few photos, a McDonalds receipt for the cheeseburgers he bought us one night on our way to the park, and a necklace. The necklace was a cheap thing, the silver chain all tarnished now and the gem hanging from it not shiny any more. But when he gave it to me, before he left for Spain, it felt as if he'd given me diamonds.

Shoebox number three was my longest relationship. It's heavy, the top barely fitting on over everything, and it's the most painful to think about. I had to put an elastic band around it to keep the lid on. It's so old now that the elastic breaks as I try to take it off.

I shriek, jumping back, but the band springs away from

me.

I pick up the photo from just inside, sighing as I look at it. With my other hand I pick up the teddy bear, his fur matted and coarse now, his body squished from being shoved inside a shoebox.

Oh, Jon. My third love.

He broke my heart worst of all.

And now I can't believe I ever wasted my time on him.

I'd spent Year Ten and Eleven trying to focus on school – I had GCSE exams, and I knew they were super-important, and I was still devastated from Ren's departure. Besides, that was when the house parties started, and I found that being single at those was fun.

The first house party took place in February half term, at some girl's house I knew from my art class, and she'd invited half the year. Most people had big brothers or sisters, or lenient parents, so there was alcohol going around. Mostly WKDs and Bacardi Breezers and beers, nothing strong, and never enough for anyone to get more than a bit tipsy – but we all acted like we were drunk from just two small bottles of beer.

And I found plenty of opportunities to kiss boys at these parties. I kissed Jon at two parties, and after the second one he asked me out. By then, it was halfway through our summer break before Sixth Form. I liked Jon: he was good-looking, nice, and a good kisser. So I said yes.

I fell for him quickly, and I fell hard. Everyone in the common room would joke that we were like an old married couple. Cathy used to ask me if I could really see myself with Jon, with her lips pursed and a worried frown, and I could. I could imagine a future with him, when he was at uni and I was doing… something.

The only problem with Jon was that he wasn't exactly faithful.

I sift through some of the photos in the box, and the folded-up notes we used to write to each other. We put them in each other's lockers for fun. He left clues to find the gifts he gave me. They'd come out of the blue, not on any particular occasion, but they were always an apology.

Lots of beaded bracelets are tangled together in the bottom of the shoebox. There's a book I never read. The teddy bear. A necklace.

Jon was more popular than I was, and he was on the rugby team. He got invited to all the parties. Sometimes I wasn't invited, or sometimes my parents just wouldn't let me go because it was a school night.

And then the next day, one of my friends would say they needed to talk to me. Either they'd been at the party, or knew someone who had been and knew all the gossip. And they'd say that so-and-so had seen Jon kissing one girl or another (it was never the same girl).

And later that morning, when I saw Jon, he'd give me whatever present he'd picked up from the shops on the walk to school, and he'd give me such a bright smile that I was sure I could make him change his wayward ways. He loved me, and I loved him. And he was obviously so very sorry – and he'd always tell me he'd drunk too much and didn't even remember it. So wasn't that okay?

I was seventeen when I decided it was time to take things further. Most people had done it already, and what was the big deal, really, they said.

'It's just sex,' I remember my friend Maggie telling me one lunchtime. I knew she'd done it plenty of times, with a couple of boys. She was *experienced*. She knew what she was talking about.

So that weekend, Jon and I went to his house while his parents were out, and that was that. I mean, it was only a matter of time anyway. We loved each other. We'd be together forever.

About two months later – a month after we'd finished our AS exams – he broke up with me.

'It's just not working,' he said.

I insisted that we could fix it, and sort out whatever wasn't working.

Then he said, 'Well, I've sort of been seeing someone else.'

I cried and shouted enough to draw the whole truth out of him. I found that for the past three months he'd been 'sort of seeing' this girl he'd met at a party from another school. She was going to university, too, unlike me. I'd already decided to drop out of Sixth Form by that point. *They* had a future together.

'She doesn't know about you,' he said. 'Please don't tell her.'

So I contacted her on Facebook later that afternoon – he'd been stupid enough to tell me her name – and told her everything. She had a right to know what kind of guy Jon was.

I put the lids back on the four shoeboxes, push them out of the way under my bed, and try to push them out of my mind, too. Maybe I was ready to try and move on from Will, but I wasn't over him yet.

I knew what Cathy would tell me to do with all this – get rid of it. Stop hanging on to bad memories.

Probably, I'd feel better about getting rid of all this stuff. I'd feel like it's a weight off my shoulders, like it's a relief, or something. It'd feel good.

Wouldn't it, at least, feel better than this nagging in the

41

pit of my stomach that just makes me feel like I'm never going to fall in love ever again?

I have some time off from my college classes over Easter, and take some time off work for a while, too. I pack up my clothes and textbooks, and go back home to see my parents for a couple of weeks.

My time off is over soon enough, and I have to go back into Cardiff for work. I only live a half hour train ride from Cardiff Central. And, for the first time since that Monday talking with Cathy, I let myself think about Sean.

I know now that he's from Swansea. But what if he stayed in Cardiff over the Easter break for work and to revise? He might have done. Maybe he is still in Cardiff. And what if he comes into Starbucks again when I'm working? What will I say to him?

From the number of times Cerys and I have spied him, we've guessed that my Starbucks is the one he usually goes to, when he's in town.

And if it is, what does that mean?

Is he going there especially to see me, or for convenience?

I start biting my nails on the train to work. I don't usually bite my nails, but I'm nervous. I can't help it.

I try to think what to do if he does show up. Do I play it cool, pretend like nothing awkward happened between us? Do I act like we're good friends now? Do I mention the kiss on the cheek?

I run a hand through my hair, and my fingers snag on a knot in my curls. I was running a bit late this morning and didn't have chance to straighten my hair. I pull the hair bobble off my wrist, and put my hair up into a ponytail.

I'm not even wearing any make-up. I have a little in my

42

bag – should I put some on in case Sean shows up?

The train pulls into Cardiff Central before I can make my mind up, and I get off, following the people from my train out through the exit, and making my way to Starbucks.

I want to see Sean again. I want to hang out with him again, not just run into him for a fleeting visit. I thought about finding him on Facebook. Cathy knows his last name so he'd be easy enough to find, but I couldn't do it. I'm not even sure if I really like him, or just let myself get swept up after he acted like my knight in shining armour on Valentine's Day.

This is why I've sworn off guys, I remind myself, when I catch myself looking in a window at my reflection to see how I look. *Because this is way too stressful.*

I'm so distracted by checking out my reflection I don't hear someone calling my name until they touch my elbow. I turn, apologising for not hearing them, and the words die on my lips.

It's Will.

He looks good. Not as good as Sean, I think, but he doesn't look bad.

'How are you?' His voice is a little breathless, like he ran to catch up to me.

'Uh…' I swallow. 'Peachy.'

'Good. Good. Um, listen, Alex, I've… I'm really glad I saw you. I've been thinking, about us, and what happened, and I think I made a huge mistake. I shouldn't have broken up with you.'

I stare at him, thinking: *It's too early in the morning for this.*

'I was thinking, maybe we could, um, give it another shot? I've been thinking about calling you for ages, but I didn't think you'd want to talk to me. I'm sorry. I'm so sorry. I shouldn't have broken up with you.'

My mind is reeling, and all I can do is gawp at him.

'Alex? Say something.'

'I'm gonna be late for work.'

Reasons I liked dating Will before

- He was sweet
- We were in love
- He went to the trouble to make big romantic gestures to show me how much he loved me

Reasons to date Will again

- I shouldn't.

Reasons not to date Will again

- It's a very, very bad idea
- I think I might finally be over him
- He lost his chance
- He broke my heart
- His eyes are too close together, he doesn't focus on life, and he's a prat
- He broke up with me on Valentine's Day
- Sean.

Chapter Six

I'm lucky that first day back at work over Easter, because I don't see Sean. It's lucky because I still haven't got my head around my talk with Will. He wants to give it another shot. He made a mistake breaking up with me.

As upset as I was over our breakup, I don't know that I want to go out with him again.

Will tries calling me, and I don't answer. Cathy tells me I'm doing the right thing, but I'm not so sure. I was in love with Will, and I did like being with him…

But I think about the list I made, and how bad an idea it would be to start dating him again.

Eventually, I decide to answer one of his calls, after almost two weeks of ignoring them. 'What do you want, Will?'

'I want to talk to you. Alex, please. I'm sorry. I'm so sorry, and I know I don't deserve another chance, but I just want to talk. Let me take you to dinner.'

Against my better judgement, and a voice in the back of my mind that sounds a lot like Cathy, I agree. Maybe I need to talk to him to get closure. So I can finally put that heartbreak behind me.

We meet up in Cardiff the next evening, and he greets me at the train station. I feel sick with nerves. It feels weird, going to dinner with Will, and not holding his hand, not giggling at something he's just said.

I look at his hand, swinging slightly at his side. Do I

want to hold that hand again?

He walks us to Bella Italia, and I stop dead outside the doors. 'You've *got* to be kidding.'

Will catches my hand before I can walk away. 'I know it's probably the last place you want to be, but I want to make things up to you. I'm trying to give you the Valentine's date we should've had together. It's romantic.'

My heart softens a little at that. It *is* a romantic gesture... and he must be serious about wanting me back if he's going to all this trouble...

When he opens the door for me, I walk inside.

And when we sit down, I have a whole other reason to be nervous.

Sean walks up to our table. I was so sure that he must've gone home to Swansea, since I haven't seen him in Starbucks for the last two weeks. I chew on my lip, looking away from him. Maybe he won't realise it's me.

He looks even better than the last time I saw him.

Seriously I didn't think it was possible, but every time I see him, he seems to get more attractive. It's like he has some kind of superpower. I think it's the glasses. It's like there's some sort of rule of the universe that attractive guys will look even better with a good pair of glasses.

'Alex?'

Crap.

I look up, and laugh awkwardly. 'Hey, Sean. It's, uh, really nice to see you.'

He looks between Will and me, and realisation dawns on his face. He bites his lip, looking away. His voice is stiff and flat when he asks what we'd like to drink. My stomach twists with guilt. I don't owe Sean anything, but I don't owe Will anything either.

I shouldn't be here.

I should, to hear what Will has to say.

He doesn't talk about us, over dinner. He doesn't talk about the girl he ditched me for on Valentine's Day, or about how badly he wants me back. I keep waiting for him to bring it up, but he still hasn't when we're halfway through our meals.

That's when I decide that enough is enough, and all the romantic gestures in the world won't make a difference. I don't love him any more.

'Will,' I say, interrupting him in the middle of a sentence, 'what are we doing?'

'What do you mean?'

'You said you wanted to talk, but we haven't actually talked. Not about *us*. And you said that you wanted to give us another shot, only I don't see why I should give you one. We can't just go back to how we were before. It's been months since we broke up. You can't just assume I'll take you back.'

Will looks at me like a wounded puppy. He reaches into his pocket, pulling out a small box and holding it out to me. 'I got you this. I'd bought it for you for Valentine's, even though we decided not to do presents, only...'

I look at the box. My hand is itching to reach out and take it, and forgive him, and give him another chance because he's really trying.

But then I look over at Sean – I catch him looking at us, and he looks away quickly, pretending to be busy. I bite my lip, turning back to Will. Just as I thought I'd got over him, he comes swanning back into my life, and even though I spent weeks after our break-up wishing for him to call me, begging me to take him back, now, I can't see why I ever wanted him back.

I let out a sharp breath, resolved. I've never dumped

48

anyone before; I've always been the one being dumped. But we're not exactly dating now, so I don't think I can call this breaking up with him.

I reach over and push his hand away. 'It's not going to happen, Will.'

'But –'

'What happened to that other girl?'

He looks away. 'Things didn't really work out. That was when I realised that I wanted you back, and I should never have ended things between us, and –'

'Stop talking, okay? You can't just take me to dinner and give me jewellery and think I'll be falling all over you. I've moved on. And I deserve better than someone who dumps me on Valentine's Day.'

I toss my napkin on the table and grab my handbag, leaving him behind like he left me.

'Alex! Wait! Alex!'

It's not Will who's chasing me out of the doors. It's Sean.

I'm tearful, and I hate myself for it. I don't want to be upset over Will again.

I expect him to start asking me what I was doing with Will, but instead he just asks, 'Are you okay?'

'Not really.' I hug my arms around myself against the cold. 'That was Will. He wanted another chance. I don't even know what I saw in him. I'm such an idiot.' I blink away some tears, and sniffle.

'You look like you need a cwtch,' Sean tells me, with a friendly smile.

I laugh, sniffling again, and let him wrap his arms around me and hold me close. He smells like Italian food and aftershave, and I hook my arms around his waist.

When I pull away from the hug, I have to wipe away

49

another tear. 'I'm sorry. I'm such a mess.'

He shakes his head. 'No you're not.'

I smile, but I'm not convinced. I glance back into the restaurant, where I can see Will throwing his fork down and running a hand through his hair, and calling to a passing waitress. I don't want to have to talk to him again. I want to be gone before he leaves the restaurant.

'I should go.'

'Need me to call you a taxi?' Sean asks, eyes twinkling.

I roll my eyes. 'Very funny.'

When I walk away from him, I'm smiling.

Chapter Seven

I'm working the next day. It's late Thursday morning, and it's slow. Cerys and I have already dissected my so-called date with Will, and are talking about her plans for her anniversary with her girlfriend next week (they're going to a cottage in St Ives) when Sean walks in.

I turn away from the door to look at Cerys, my eyes as wide as they can go. Her eyes are just as wide, and the only difference in our expressions is that she's smiling.

'Shut up,' I hiss, but she only stifles a giggle. I turn back so I'm facing the counter, trying my best to look calm and collected. Sean's still in the doorway, looking for a table – or at least pretending to – and he's with two other guys.

The other guys, who I guess are his mates, look at me in a way that they probably think is subtle, but isn't, and then they look at each other, raising eyebrows and pulling faces. Sean turns to them, pointing at a table.

After last night, I don't know what I should say to him. That's the second time he's comforted me, and I don't know how to thank him for it. I also don't know if he did it because he cares about me, or just because he's a nice guy.

One of the guys glances back over at me, and I stare down at my nails, trying to look as if I'm not bothered by any of this. I really need to sort out my cuticles, I think, getting distracted. Then they're standing in front of me.

'Hi,' says Sean.

'Hi.' My voice gives me away – it comes out squeaky and nervous. I clear my throat. 'What can I get you?'

'I'll have a medium latte,' says one of his mates, pushing Sean aside. Is it just a coincidence that they've all come here when I'm working? I can't tell. Are they here acting like wingmen?Or are they just trying to make Sean feel awkward?

I sort out the latte, and the other guy's large mocha and a cookie, and they go off to a table on the other side of the room, leaving me at the counter with Sean. Cerys announces that she's going to clean some tables and make sure there's enough milk out. I grab her arm but she shrugs me off.

Leaving me and Sean, effectively, alone.

I'm not nervous. I don't have any reason to be nervous.

'So,' I say, after drawing in a deep breath. 'What can I get you?'

'Latte, please. Medium.'

'Any goodies?' I gesture at the glass case of cakes and sweet things.

'Are you on the menu?' He winks, and I can't help but burst out laughing.

I say, 'Sean, are you flirting with me?'

His grin is mischievous. 'Sorry, but you left that line open for the taking. I couldn't resist.'

'So no cakes?'

'No cakes.'

I put it through the till, and as I'm making the latte, I say to Sean, trying my best to be casual, 'Did you, um, did you go back home for the holidays?'

'Yeah, but I came back a couple of days ago. It's a bit easier to revise here. A little more peace and quiet, and

52

I'm working, too, so…'

'Yeah. Fair enough.'

'How about you?'

'Oh, I'm not that far away. It's not long on the train to come into work, or if they want me on the early shift, I can stay in the house here rather than at home. But that's kind of lonely, because none of the girls are back yet. Their uni term doesn't start again for a little while.'

He nods, and I push the latte across the counter to him. I don't let go of it before he wraps his hand around the cup – so around my hand, too. I blush, and my hand starts to sweat. Only I can't take it away and wipe it on my trousers. That would be even more embarrassing. Oh, man, I hope he can't tell my palms are sweating.

I look up from the latte and our hands to see Sean studying my face. He meets my eyes. I gulp.

'Are you still hung up on that guy from last night?'

'Actually, I think I'm finally over him. Last night was just… closure. I mean, I thought I loved him, but now I'm starting to think that I just fell for all the romantic gestures, you know? I know it sounds shallow, but…'

'It doesn't sound shallow.'

'I'm over him,' I say, sure of it now. I told Cathy the same last night, over the phone, when I got home, and she was totally speechless. She said that it looked like I might be growing up.

'In that case…' The corner of Sean's lips twist up. 'What would you say to going out to dinner with me?'

I'm totally thrown. He's blushing a little, and I think I must be, too.

I want to say yes, so badly. But I think about every reason I have to say no, and all the times my heart has already been broken, and I know what my answer should

53

be.

I sigh. 'Sean…'

'Or we could just go for coffee – only I thought you have enough of that here. We could go for drink somewhere? If you'd like?'

I stare at him a little longer, speechless.

'Like, on a date,' he clarifies.

'Oh. Right. Um, of course.'

Like I didn't already know that's what you meant.

'Of course as in of course you'll go out with me?' His voice is bright, and hopeful. So is his smile. That wonderful, gorgeous smile.

'Sean, I… I don't think it's such a good idea.'

'If you really don't fancy me, or whatever, then tell me. It's okay. I'm a big boy, I can take it.' He's joking, but it's half-hearted.

'No, it's not that. Look, this isn't the best time. What with trying to keep on top of my coursework, and my job, I've got enough on my plate without starting a new relationship, you know? I'm sorry.'

I don't mention that, knowing my luck, any relationship wouldn't go anywhere anyway. Sean's in his final year of his degree. He might do his teacher training somewhere else. I might never see him again after his exams, if he goes back home for the summer and then goes somewhere else to become a teacher.

We're just not meant to be.

Because even though we keep running into each other, there's no such thing as fate.

The more I think about dating Sean, the more I convince myself it'll end in heartbreak, and the more I convince myself I'm jinxed when it comes to romance.

Sean smiles at me. 'That's okay. I understand. Your

college class is important, and it's great that you're working so hard at it.'

'I'm sorry. I really am.'

'Don't be. I understand.'

And from the genuine smile still on his face, I believe he does.

'Well,' he says then, reaching for a napkin from the pile nearby, 'give me a pen. I'll give you my number, and if you want a break from revision and work – a cup of tea, a few pints, whatever, then give me a call, and we can hang out. As mates, yeah?'

I hand him the pen we use to write on the takeaway cups, and he carefully writes out his mobile number for me. I take it, and he takes his latte. 'Thanks.'

'Seriously, any time. Just let me know.'

'I will,' I promise him. 'I will.'

I don't.

I don't call him, that is, because I'm not that stupid.

I know how this would work out: we'd start hanging out as mates, and then we'd grow close quickly, and end up kissing, then going on a couple of casual dates, then we'd sleep together because I'd be head over heels for him, and then things will break down and he'll break my heart. Just like all the others.

So even though a couple of times I type out a text to him about meeting up for drinks later in the evening, or grabbing lunch somewhere to catch up, I don't go through with it. I delete the texts and toss my phone aside. And I definitely don't call him.

'I want to, don't get me wrong,' I tell Cathy over the phone. I've got my mobile tucked between my cheek and my shoulder, and I hunch over in my desk chair in my room, painting my toenails. They're a fierce, bright blue. 'But…'

'I've gotta be honest, I really didn't think you were serious about this whole no-dating thing. You cried over that movie, *John Tucker Must Die*, for Christ's sake. You cried over Mitch and Cam's wedding in *Modern Family*. You're hopeless for romance.'

'Are you always going to bring that up?'

'You know it.'

I sigh, and say, 'Look, I just know this is never going to work. I'm trying to be sensible and save myself the heartache.'

'And you're missing out on a lot of fun in the meantime. Come on, he's a nice guy! Why don't you just go out as friends? Make it a group thing. I'll come along, and you can get

him to bring some mates, too. And then even if you two don't get together, maybe I'll hook up with one of his mates.'

She laughs, and I roll my eyes, because she can't see me do it. 'I told you. I can't *just* be friends with him.'

'Please, you haven't even tried!'

'He is *literally* everything I could want in a guy. Smart. Good-looking. Funny. Nice. Lives kind of near. Has an idea of what he wants to do with his life. I cannot hang out with a guy like that and not fall for him.'

'If he's so perfect, then –'

I groan. 'We're going round in circles. Can we just not talk about Sean any more, please?'

'Fine,' she mumbles. 'But you brought him up.'

'Are you definitely coming back to the house tomorrow?' The girls have exams coming up soon. Julia's on holiday and won't be back here for a week yet, and

56

Ellie's coming back on Wednesday, on the train. I've only been here a couple of days on my own, but it already feels lonely.

'Of course I am.' We start talking about how we need to buy more soap and bleach for the house bathroom, and whether Cathy should take a break from revision with a girly movie night with me later this week.

She tries to bring up the subject of Sean again, but I avoid it. All the talk of Sean, and relationships, is making me think about what a mess all my other relationships have been.

I look under my bed, thinking about the train-wreck that is my love life history, and I'm distracted for the rest of the call.

After I hang up the phone, and finish painting my toes, I reach underneath my bed and pull out the four shoeboxes there.

I take the lids off and look inside them, thinking about the four guys who broke my heart. And I think, I deserve better than to hang on to all this crap.

I grab the oldest shoebox. I suck in a deep breath, and upturn the box into my bin.

I pick up the second box.

I'm purging, I tell myself. I'm getting rid of all this bad energy. The next shoebox gets emptied into my bin, too.

Maybe I should have burned all of this a long time ago, I think, looking at the now empty shoeboxes and my overflowing bin. Maybe burning it would make me feel better.

Then there's the final shoebox, with everything from my relationship with Will. The heart necklace he gave me is on the top, catching the light. I remember how happy I was when he gave it to me. How in love I was.

I've always believed in love. In romance. In butterflies in my stomach telling me *he's The One!* and that feeling so strong and so consuming that it could only be love.

Now, the necklace clatters as it knocks against the metal of my bin. It's a satisfying sort of sound.

Looking at all the crap in my bin, I start thinking that maybe I never actually loved any of them, not really. I got caught up in the romance, but that's not the same.

I didn't feel whatever I feel for Sean for any of the others.

And if I'm being honest with myself, whatever I do feel for Sean scares me.

Chapter Eight

Without any warning, Cathy bursts into my room. She's wearing her dressing gown, and holds up two dresses for me to see. One is a little black bodycon, and the other is bright blue, silky, with white flowers on.

Cathy rarely asks for second opinions on her outfits. She's so self-confident – I've always admired her for it. So I immediately know that something is up.

'Why do you look so stressed out?'

'I *don't* look stressed out. Do I?' She throws the dresses on my bed and leans down to my desk mirror to inspect her face. She's frowning, so I don't think she can argue with me. My best friend takes a deep breath before picking her dresses back up.

'Okay. Which one?'

'Why are you getting so worked up? I thought it was just a house party.'

When she told me earlier that there was a party some guy had invited her to, and she didn't want to chill out watching a cheesy chick flick or reading Sherlock fanfiction again, she'd been really upbeat. 'I need a break from revision. I wake up in the middle of the night reeling off German grammar. I need a break, Alex, and you're coming with me. And don't say no, because you haven't got any classes tomorrow, and you're not working, either, so you have no excuses.'

Now, I get it.

The guy who's invited her.

That's why she's freaking out about what to wear.

'*Ohmigod*,' I exclaim. 'There's a guy. Spill.'

She blushes. 'He's just a guy. I mean, a friend. You know? He just asked me because he was being polite. We were talking about revision and he mentioned that the guys in his house were having a party, so invited me. Us. That's all.'

'Right,' I scoff, not believing it for a second. 'So you don't like him at all?'

She laughs, throwing her head back. 'Oh, I didn't say *that*.'

I laugh too, and tell her to wear the blue dress – it makes her boobs look good, and doesn't show as much skin as the black one. 'Classy *is* sexy,' I say.

Cathy goes back to her room to dress, and I pick out something from my own wardrobe to wear. I doubt I'll know anyone there – I'm only really going for Cathy – and I'm not out to impress anyone, either. I go for a plain pink jersey dress with a skirt that swings around my knees and sleeves to my elbows, and pair it with some ankle boots.

I learnt after one unfortunate incident, when a girl behind me threw up, that sandals are hardly ever a good idea at a house party.

The neckline is low on my dress, and I rummage through my tangled collection of necklaces before going to Cathy's room to look through hers.

After I picked one out with a big, oval stone that's deep black and shiny, Cathy asks me to help curl her hair. She doesn't usually go to the effort, so this guy must be something special.

I stand behind her at her desk, with curling tongs, and we look at each other's reflections in her mirror as we chat.

'I'm so jealous of your hair, Al,' she sighs. My thick, dark hair hangs in unruly waves to my shoulders. I see that it's actually bordering on frizzy, despite all the mousse I used. I'd usually straighten it, but tonight I can't be bothered. It's not like I've got anybody to impress at this party.

I lift a section of Cathy's silky blonde hair. 'At least your hair doesn't need ten different products to keep it under control.'

We walk to the house, since it's not far away and neither of us is wearing heels, and show up around nine o'clock. The house is three storeys, tall and thin, but it's bursting with activity. There are a few people sitting on the pavement outside smoking and as we walk past, I smell that it's pot they're smoking, not cigarettes.

We push past people clustered in the doorway to get into the house, and find that the party is in full swing. There's music coming from the kitchen and different music coming from the living room, and people on the stairs either snogging or just chatting and drinking.

I don't see anybody I know, and glance at Cathy. She looks just as lost as I do.

I look at Cathy. 'What now?'

She bites her lip, a determined look on her face, still looking around. I can guess who she's looking for.

'Maybe he's in the kitchen?' I suggest, and she nods. We make our way through, and take the opportunity to sort ourselves out some drinks – lemonade for me, and a glass of wine for Cathy. While we stand there sipping our drinks, Cathy scans the crowd.

We don't have any luck there, or in the living room, or

the dining room, but we do find him in the garden. He looks familiar, but I can't think where I've seen him. Cathy introduces us.

'Alex, this is Simon. Simon, this is my best friend, Alex, the one I told you about.'

We say hi to each other, and Simon looks at me funny – like he recognises me as well, but can't remember where he's seen me before. I think about asking him, but Cathy puts a hand on Simon's bicep and starts telling him what a great party it is, and how grateful she is for the break from revision.

I linger for a couple of minutes, mostly silent. They talk and joke like they've known each other forever. From the way that Cathy's face lights up when he smiles at her, I decide that maybe I should give them some time alone.

In fact I feel like a complete third wheel already, and they're barely touching.

'I'm just, um… I'm going to go to the bathroom,' I say, finally finding an excuse.

Cathy's eyes flicker back to me briefly, and I see a pang of guilt there. She feels bad that she brought me to this party and now she's ditched me for a boy. But it's okay. That's what best friends are for, right?

I'll just mingle for a while.

'I'll see you later,' I tell her, with a smile. To Simon, I add, 'It was nice to meet you.'

'Yeah, you too.' He looks pretty glad that I'm leaving them alone.

I weave through the ground floor of the house, smiling at people I don't know and somehow getting into a conversation with a group of people about a band playing at the Motorpoint Arena in a couple of weeks.

After a while, I try to find Cathy again, but I can't see

her anywhere.

I hope she's having a good time with Simon, if she's still with him.

I find somewhere to put my empty glass down, and search instead for a bathroom. There's one on the ground floor, but there's a long queue of people. The longer I wait, the more I realise how desperate I am.

There has to be a bathroom upstairs.

I totally understand that whoever is renting this house might not want people going upstairs, but I have a feeling they won't really mind. It's not like I'm looking for a bedroom to snog a guy in privacy, and I won't throw up and make a mess.

So I pick my way between all the people on the stairs. None of them stop me and tell me I shouldn't go up, so I guess I must be getting away with it. Which is good, because I am *busting*.

I find a bathroom on the top floor – the door is open, so I go right in and lock it behind me. Once I'm done, I open the door back up, and find someone standing on the other side.

I catch the surprised expression on the guy's face, and guess he must live here. I look away quickly, embarrassed. I feel like I've been caught by a parent or something. Like he's about to tell me off for coming upstairs.

I'm about to apologise, when he says, 'Alex?'

I look up, startled. And say, 'You have *got* to be kidding me.'

I don't mean to say it out loud, but it's too late to take it back. Sean's eyebrows shoot up.

Of course it's him. Of *course*.

I should've been expecting this. I mean, I always bump into him at the most awkward times, so why not now?

63

All I can think to say then is, 'I'm sorry for using the upstairs bathroom.'

Sean just laughs.

I blush, beyond embarrassed. 'It's okay,' he says. 'You don't look like you were causing trouble.'

'Oh, no more than usual.' I grin, and then remember that this is a bad idea and that I shouldn't be flirting with him. But hard as I try, I can't wipe the smile off my face.

He leans sideways against the doorframe, giving me space to walk out of the bathroom. I could go downstairs, but I don't. My feet won't carry me there. Instead, I stop opposite him, under the doorframe. I have to crane my neck to meet his eyes.

As I drag my eyes up to his, I take in what he's wearing. Worn joggers that are falling apart at the hems, bare feet, and a hoodie with a school badge on that says 'Leavers 2010'. His hair is messy and he's wearing his glasses. He's not dressed for a party.

He's not *at* the party, I realise.

He lives here. This is his house. His housemates are throwing this party.

That's why Simon looked so familiar! He's come into Starbucks before with Sean!

If I had recognised him earlier maybe I wouldn't be so tongue-tied right now in front of Sean.

God. Just as I thought it couldn't get worse.

I try to remind myself that this is a very, very bad idea. After I made it clear to Sean that I wasn't after a relationship and rejected him, he won't be interested in me. If he were, he'd have invited me, right?

'What're you doing here?' he asks, when I don't go anywhere.

'My friend Cathy, she – your friend Simon invited her,

and she brought me along. Only I kind of lost her, because she was talking to Simon, and I was being a third-wheel, so I left. And there was a queue for the bathroom downstairs, so…'

I'm babbling. I shut up before I say anything that will make me even more mortified.

Sean smiles. 'I didn't realise the girl Simon was talking about was your friend Cathy.'

What's that supposed to mean? That maybe if he'd known, he'd have invited me as well, if only to be polite?

I chew on my bottom lip, because I don't know what to say.

Sean rubs the back of his neck, and says, 'If I'd known you were coming, I'd probably have gone downstairs. Once they decided to throw a party, there was no stopping them. But I wasn't really in the mood.'

'Why not?'

He shrugs, just the one shoulder. 'I wanted to finish writing up notes. Revision. You know.'

'Yeah.' I wonder if he's saying that to get rid of me, not just to answer my question. 'Well, I guess, um, maybe I should leave you to it. Revision, I mean.'

I make my way to the top of the stairs, wondering if I should try to find Cathy again or just go home, when Sean calls my name.

'I'm not trying to be rude, but do you actually know anyone here?'

'What, aside from you, Cathy, and your mate Simon?' I smile, but it feels stiff, so I stop. 'Not really.'

'It's just,' he says, 'I finished the notes I was working on and I was going to relax for a bit with a movie. The new *Thor*. It's not like I can get any sleep with this lot.' He makes a wide gesture, obviously talking about the party going on downstairs. 'You could watch it with me, if you want?'

Before I can even think about whether it's a good idea, I say, 'I love *Thor*.'

Chapter Nine

What am I doing?

I'm crazy. I've totally lost it. That's the only explanation.

Sean is clearing papers off his bed, sorting them into an open ring-binder file. His bed is against the wall, facing his desk where he's got a TV and an Xbox.

I'm going to have to sit on his bed.

I'm about to sit on Sean's bed.

It might be just to watch a movie, and totally innocent, but it doesn't matter. It's still weird. Intimate. And it's not like we're even really friends, so what does that make us? Are we friends now, and just hanging out? Or is this something... *more*?

God, I wish I knew. Sean moves the file to his desk, and loads a DVD into his Xbox. And the longer I stand in his room, with the door shut behind me, the more I start to think this is a terrible idea. If I stay here, sitting on his bed, next to him, I'm going to kiss him.

Hell, he's a good-looking guy. I'm only human.

I can't do this.

I can't get my heart broken again.

Sean must see something in my face that gives me away. 'Is everything okay, Alex?'

Much as I want to say yes, I shake my head. 'I'm sorry. I – I should go. I really can't do this. I'm sorry.'

'What? What's wrong? Did – did I do something?'

'No! No, it's not…' *It's not you, it's me.* I can't say that. 'I'm sorry if I've been leading you on, Sean, I really am, but this is… It's too much.'

He edges closer, by just a step. I bite my lip again. I have the opportunity to hang out (and probably snog) the perfect guy, and I'm backing out. I am definitely crazy.

And maybe just a little bit sensible.

'Alex, hey,' he says softly, 'talk to me. You know you can talk to me.'

'That's the thing – I *don't* know. I hardly know you, Sean. You helped me out of a tight spot and then we bumped into each other a few times. And we might've talked a lot at McDonalds, but it's…'

I trail off, feeling stupid and pathetic.

I keep thinking of all the lists I made – about why I should stop dating, and why dating Sean would be a bad idea, but now all the points on those lists blur together in my mind until I can't remember what they said.

Sean's eyebrows knit together behind his glasses. 'Alex. Come on.'

The look he gives me is one that says, *Tell me the truth, and stop bullshitting around.*

So I do.

'I'm jinxed,' I blurt.

'Jinxed? What, like, bad luck?' I can see him fighting back a smirk, but try not to let it annoy me.

'My love life, I mean. Every guy I've ever been out with has broken my heart and you can't tell me that this won't go the same way. I mean, have you *met* you? You're perfect. You were my knight in shining armour right from the start.'

He blushes, ducking his head to look at his feet. But he's smiling.

'And let's face it, Sean, any relationship we have is over before it starts. It's not like either of us has the time, and then you'll move back to Swansea. And then you'll be getting on with your teaching stuff and move somewhere else for a job, and…' I sigh. 'I'm sorry, but I can't be *just friends* with you.'

Time seems to slow to almost a total stop. Sean drags his gaze up to meet mine sooooo slowly, and it feels like he sets all my nerves on fire. I'm burning up from the inside just from that one look.

Sean straightens up, and leans closer. It's only a slight movement, but makes him tower over me. I forget how to breathe. I hope he doesn't kiss me. I feel so alive, so electric, that I'm sure I'll shatter into a million pieces if he kisses me. I won't be able to handle more than this.

I've been in love plenty of times before, but not one of those guys could make me feel like this with just a look.

The gold flecks in Sean's eyes seem brighter, more noticeable, and they make it look like his eyes are full of flames. I'm tempted to let my gaze drop down his body and take in every inch of him, but my eyes are glued to his.

I have never wanted a guy to both kiss me and not kiss me more in my entire life.

Then, after a painfully long silence, he says in a whisper, 'You know, I'm coming back here to do my PGCE.'

And what will that give me, I wonder, a year, two years? It wouldn't be enough.

I don't give my heart over lightly. With me, it's all or nothing, and always has been. And with Sean… He'll break my heart worse than anyone else.

I don't realise I've said all that aloud until he steps

closer, and says, 'Maybe. But isn't it better than regretting that you didn't?'

My mouth falls open, but no words come out. I hesitate.

I shouldn't have come to this party. I should've stayed home. Far away from Sean.

But everywhere I go, I run into him. In work, on nights out, here… I can't get away from him. It's like – like the universe is throwing us together all the time, and no matter how many times I try to run away, I'll still be running towards him.

Almost like there *is* such a thing as fate.

The romantic in me is back, and she's here to stay, I realise.

So now, the way I see it, I have two choices – keep running, or stand still.

His hand on my face startles me, and I blink, focusing back on Sean. His thumb skims over my cheekbone. His skin is cool, but his touch sets my whole body on fire again. And I'm leaning into him, head tilting up, almost automatically.

I can see hope flickering in his eyes, but there's tension in the rest of his face, like he can't let himself hope too much. Because he thinks I'll reject him again. He's sure I will.

But he has to ask me.

'So?' he breathes. 'What's it gonna be?'

I'm standing still. I'm not running any more.

In answer, I kiss him.

This kiss isn't on the cheek. Sean is still for a moment. Shocked, I guess. But just as I start to pull away, his arm wraps around me and the hand he's got on my cheek slips around to the back of my head, knotting into my hair. And he's kissing me back in a way that makes me think I've

70

never really been kissed before.

It's intense and desperate and so, so gentle, all at once. I don't melt in his arms, though – I push back into him with everything I've got, hoping that time doesn't start moving again. This is something I never want to end.

But it does – my clutch bag starts vibrating at my feet. When did I drop my bag? And when did Sean press me up against the door?

We pull apart and I bend down to get my phone. Sean steps back, giving me space, and I look up at him with a guilty smile. 'I'm sorry, it's Cathy… I should get this.'

I answer, but before I can get out a hello, she shrieks, 'Where the hell are you? Did you go home? Are you at home? I've been looking all over for you and I can't find you! Where are you?'

She's so loud that I have to pull the phone away from my ear. That's when I see the three texts she's sent me that I've missed. All in the last ten minutes, all asking where I am.

'Calm down,' I say. 'I'm still here.'

'Well where the hell are you?'

'I'm with Sean.'

There's a long pause.

'Alexandra Singh, I am only going to ask you one question, and I want an honest answer. Are you naked right now?'

'No!' I sound really shrill, and I blush. 'God, Cathy.'

'Sorry, just checking. So what are you doing, just hanging out with him?'

'Sort of.'

'Please tell me I haven't *interrupted* something,' she groans.

'No, Cathy! Jeez. We're just…'

71

'If that sentence isn't PG, don't finish it.'

'Kissing,' I mumble.

There's another long pause.

Then a scream – a scream I'm pretty sure I can hear from within the house and not just from the phone. 'What does this mean? Are you two together?'

She reels off more questions, and I say over the top of them, 'Cathy. Cathy. Cathy,' until she stops.

'I'm upstairs with Sean and we're gonna watch a movie. When you're ready to leave, give me another call, and we'll head home. Okay? And I'll talk to you then.'

'Okay.'

'Okay.'

I hang up, and turn my mobile off silent, so that when she rings again later, I'll hear it. Sean's sitting on his bed now – on the edge, his hands beside his thighs – and raises his eyebrows.

'She was wondering where I was.'

'Ah.'

He probably heard the whole conversation because, let's face it, Cathy's a loud drunk, even on the phone. But I'm too nervous to ask, in case he didn't hear. I'd rather pretend he didn't know.

Because that'd be pretty embarrassing.

Instead, I sit on the bed next to Sean, and say, 'So, are we watching this movie, or not?'

A couple of hours later, when the credits are rolling and I'm combing through my tousled hair with my fingers before I go to meet Cathy downstairs, I realise just how much I don't want to leave Sean. I could stay here and cwtch up with him forever.

My intense work ethic for college is so going out the

window with him around.

'Um, so, you… do you still have my number? From when I gave it to you in Starbucks? Wait, no, what am I saying, of course you don't. You probably threw it away. Shall I – shall I give you my number?'

'I have it,' I say quietly, with a smile. I love how nervous he gets, like he's terrified of saying the wrong thing and making me change my mind about him. On anyone else it'd be annoying – but on him, it's endearing.

'You do?'

Should I be offended at how shocked he is? Do I come across as such a cold bitch?

'I do.'

'Oh. Right. Well.'

'I thought about texting you. Lots of times. But – I was too scared.'

'Scared I'd break your heart?'

'Well, yeah.' I blush. When he says it that way, it makes me sound like a stupid little girl who thinks real life is all some fairy tale.

Sean's fingertips graze over my hot, pink cheeks, and I glance up through my eyelashes to see him smiling at me. It's a beautiful smile. His eyes are lit up and his eyes crinkle at the corners, and it makes me feel good inside. Like I should be smiling, too.

'Call me tomorrow, then,' he says. 'Or, you know, whenever. The day after, if you're too busy. But – text me, when you get home? So I know you're back safe.'

I kiss him again. I could spend a lifetime kissing Sean. 'I will.'

When I get to the bedroom door, I realise that Sean's hanging back. I look over my shoulder at him. He's looking at his feet, at his wiggling toes, and his hands are locked on top of his head.

'Alex?'

'Yeah?'

'You're not going to change your mind, are you?'

At this point, I realise that Sean likes me a lot. A lot more than I thought he did.

'Definitely not. Remember – it's all or nothing with me.'

He smiles. 'I'd be happy with just a little bit of you, as long as it was more than nothing.'

It's hardly a great vote for romance, but the way it makes me feel so warm and fuzzy, he might as well have said he loves me.

Epilogue

'Congratulations!'

I turn around to see Sean beaming at me, and he wraps me in a hug that lifts me off my feet. I laugh, giddy with excitement, and lean my face down to kiss him.

It's graduation day for me. The sun is shining, which makes a nice change from all the recent drizzle. And Sean is here. It's a perfect day.

Sean sets me back on my feet, stroking my hair back over my shoulder, where the wind has blown it out of place. I grin up at him, hardly believing that I've made it here – not just to university, but to graduation, leaving with a two-one degree in psychology.

He kisses me again, and I shiver all the way down my spine. I will never get used to kissing him. I'm still not used to it after all these years. There are butterflies in my stomach that have nothing to do with graduating and everything to do with my boyfriend.

My boyfriend.

I'll never get used to calling Sean my boyfriend, either.

I cup his face in my hands now. His cheeks are rough with stubble, and pink from the wind. Even though it's sunny, it's not particularly warm.

Sean's teaching French in a comprehensive school not too far away. And I've got a job in the Human Resources department at the local offices of a car insurance firm. I start next month. I'll only be covering maternity leave, but they've said they're hoping to expand the department, so I'm keeping my fingers crossed.

Everything is working out for us.

The romantic in me is certain that the entire universe has been rooting for the two of us right from the start.

'What are you thinking about?' Sean asks me, noticing the faraway look in my eyes.

'That I'm glad you were my waiter at Bella Italia that night, when I got dumped. It must've been fate.'

Sean chuckles. I feel it through his chest, where my hands are braced against him now. He's used to me saying things like this, talking about us like we're from a Nicholas Sparks novel or something.

'Fate, huh?'

'Fate,' I say, with more certainty. 'It has to be. That I met you in the restaurant that night, that you came into my Starbucks… Every time I met you at first was by chance. I'm telling you, that's fate.'

He kisses me. 'I love you.'

'I love you, too.'

I'll never get used to saying that, either.

Cathy comes running over then, pushing Sean out of the way to throw her arms around me. 'Ooh, I'm so happy for you, Alex! Well done!'

'Thanks.' I grin at her.

'I told you, you could do it, didn't I?' Her voice is a mix of proud and smug. Her blonde hair is tied up in a pretty bun, and she's smiling as widely as I am. Cathy's had a few boyfriends on and off over the last couple of years, and she's single now. But it doesn't seem to bother her – and she's not even a little bit jealous that I've found The One for me.

Because I'm sure he is – I'm sure that Sean is the only

one I'll ever want again. He's everything and more I could ask for in a boyfriend.

We're even getting a flat together.

Which is pretty damn serious as far as my parents are concerned. 'Serious enough,' my mum stated, when I told her the news. 'I'm only fifty two, Alex. You'd better not surprise me with grandchildren any time soon.'

'God, Mum!' I cried, and she hmmph-ed one last time and dropped the subject.

Now, I steal a glance at Sean as Cathy starts talking a mile a minute about the trip to Germany she's got planned for the summer as an au-pair. He smiles at me, looking at me like I'm his entire world. I know, because that's how I look at him.

And I couldn't be happier.

Quick Reads 2015

My Sporting Heroes – Jason Mohammad
Captain Courage – Gareth Thomas
Code Black: Winter of Storm Surfing – Tom
Anderson
Cwtch Me if You Can – Beth Reekles

For more information about **Quick Reads**

and other **Accent Press** titles

please visit

www.accentpress.co.uk